Spider Storch, Rotten Runner

Gina Willner-Pardo
illustrated by Nick Sharratt

Albert Whitman & Company • Morton Grove, Illinois

01 3895

Library of Congress Cataloging-in-Publication Data

Willner-Pardo, Gina.
Spider Storch, rotten runner / by Gina Willner-Pardo;
illustrated by Nick Sharratt.
p. cm.
Summary: Although he knows just about everything about spiders,
Spider Storch is a terrible runner, and he's afraid he'll ruin the
Third-Grade Olympics for his teammates.
ISBN: 0-8075-7594-1 (hardcover)
[1. Running — Fiction. 2. Teamwork (Sports) — Fiction.
3. Schools — Fiction. 4. Friendship — Fiction.]
I. Sharratt, Nick, ill. II. Title.
PZ7.W683675 Spb 2001 [Fic] — dc21
2001001238

Designed by Scott Piehl.

To faithful readers Jesse and
Casey Baldridge, and, as always,
to Evan and Cara. — G.W.-P.

For Graham Byers and
Frank Jepson. — N.S.

Don't forget to read . . .

Spider Storch's
Teacher Torture

Spider Storch's
Carpool Catastrophe

Spider Storch's
Music Mess

Spider Storch's
Fumbled Field Trip

Spider Storch's
Desperate Deal

by Gina Willner-Pardo

illustrated by Nick Sharratt

Contents

1

1

Olympic Fever

P.E. is my favorite part of school.
Mr. Hudson says it stands for
"physical education," but all I know
is you don't have to sit at a desk and
there aren't any wrong answers.

This is especially good for me,
because at school I am wrong a lot,
and I hate being wrong.

Mr. Hudson is the P.E. teacher at

my school. Ms. Schmidt is my teacher for third grade, but she can't teach P.E., probably because her fingernails are too long. When my class has P.E. on Wednesdays and Fridays, Ms. Schmidt goes to the teachers' lounge.

No kids have ever been in the teachers' lounge. That's where the principal keeps the dead bodies of all the kids who got strangled or drowned on school property.

"There aren't any dead bodies in the teachers' lounge," Zachary whispered. We were sitting in a big circle on the playground. We were waiting for Mr. Hudson to stop writing on his clipboard. "That's just a story that someone made up."

"Yeah," Andrew whispered back. "That's just something the first-graders think."

"But don't you think it's weird that no kid has ever been in there?" I said.

"My mom has a walk-in closet and I'm not allowed in there," Zachary said.

"And what about all the kids who've just disappeared?" I said. "*Mysteriously* disappeared. Like that fifth-grader who ate too many French fries in the cafeteria. They took her

away to pump her stomach and no one ever saw her again. Or Wallace O'Neil. Remember him?"

"I heard he got a heart attack from doing jumping jacks," Andrew said. "And the paramedics tried to shock his heart, but he got electrocuted instead."

"I heard he got asthma and had to move to Arizona," Zachary said.

"I don't know," I said. I did kind of wonder. "It wouldn't surprise me one bit if they kept a big box of dead kids in the back of a closet in the teachers' lounge."

"How come they don't smell?" Andrew asked. "Dead bodies usually smell."

"Maybe Mr. Scruggs soaks them in something," I said. Mr. Scruggs is the janitor. "Maybe that's what's in all those bottles he carries around on his cart."

"Mr. Hudson!" Mary Grace Brennerman was waving her hand in the air. "Joey and Andrew and Zachary are talking about dead kids."

Mr. Hudson looked up from his clipboard. I liked him because he knew a lot about P.E., and because he wasn't like Mrs. Troutman, the last P.E. teacher we had. She smelled like the back of a closet and made us do folk dancing with the girls.

Mr. Hudson wasn't like that. He did some dumb things, like make us run twice around the playground, even in the rain. And he made us stretch, which isn't even exercise. But most of the time, he was a pretty good guy.

"Thanks a lot for the update,

Mary Grace," he said. "Okay, guys. Ready for a news flash?"

I liked that Mr. Hudson didn't even pay attention when Mary Grace tried to get us in trouble.

"Get ready for—" Mr. Hudson spread out his arms "—the Third-Grade Olympics! Does everyone watch the Olympics on TV?"

Everyone yelled yes, except for Rose Marie Newman, whose parents don't believe in TV. They make Rose Marie read the newspaper instead.

"What's your favorite event?" Mr. Hudson asked the class.

"BOBSLEDDING!" I yelled. I forgot about waiting to be called on.

A lot of people said ice-skating and diving and gymnastics. Travis Hoffberg liked soccer and

skiing. Mary Grace liked ballroom
dancing.

"Ballroom dancing!" I said. "That's
not a sport! That's *dancing!*"

Mary Grace can be so dumb.
Zachary and Andrew and I all looked
at each other and shook our heads.

Regina Littlefield raised her hand.

"Track and field," she said. "That's
my favorite! I like the racing. The way
they run so fast!"

"Yeah!" Zachary said. "I like when
they show it in slow motion. You can

see their muscles bulging
in their legs."

Everyone started
talking about racing.

I kept quiet. I didn't see why everyone
thought running was such a big deal.

"Runners are the best athletes,"
Zachary said. "Carl Lewis won four
Olympic gold medals, just like Jesse
Owens."

"Actually, he won nine gold medals
altogether," I said. "He won four in
one Olympics."

I may not like to run, but I know a
lot about famous runners. I know a lot
about sports in general. I know more
than Zachary does.

Mr. Hudson said, "Joey's right,
Zachary. And Lewis won a silver
medal, too."

"But—" Zachary said.

"In the two-hundred meter," I said.

Zachary gave me a dirty look.

Before Zachary could say anything more, Mr. Hudson held up his hands.

"Okay, *okay*. I'm still working out some of the details. On Friday, I'll let you know the events you'll be competing in. Ms. Schmidt is going to help you pick out the country you're going to represent."

"Can't we just be the boys against the girls?" Andrew asked.

Mr. Hudson shook his head. "There are four third-grade classes, and each one is going to represent a different country. I want you to start thinking of your classmates as your teammates. I want you to root for each other and help each other out."

Oh, brother, I thought.

On the way back to Room Six, Zachary kept talking about racing.

"I'm a really fast runner," he said.

"Me, too," Andrew said.

I didn't say anything.

"We're going to beat all the other third grades," Andrew said. "With us and Regina Littlefield, no one can beat us."

"We should pick a really cool country to be," Zachary said. "How about Madagascar?"

"That's not a real country," I said. "How about Australia? The funnel-web spider lives in Australia."

"Madagascar is *so* a real country," Zachary said. "And it has fast runners."

"So?" I was getting sick of all this talk about running. "I don't see why we have to pick a country just because it has fast runners."

Zachary was giving me a funny look.

"Especially a made-up country like Madagascar," I said.

"It's not made up!" Zachary yelled. "It's an island right next to Africa!"

"Australia's better for a team," I said. "People don't want to be a country no one's ever heard of before."

"How do you know?" Zachary asked.

"*Everybody* knows that," I said.

That was what I said to get people
to stop arguing with me.

Zachary didn't say anything else.
He didn't look too sure about
Madagascar, though.

2

Go, France, Go

"How was P.E.?" Ms. Schmidt asked.

She looked more wide awake than she did during Math, which we had right before P.E. Maybe she took a nap in the teachers' lounge. Or maybe not, with all those dead kids in there.

Mary Grace started explaining about picking a country.

"Thank you very much, Mary Grace. Mr. Hudson told me all about the Third-Grade Olympics." Ms. Schmidt picked up a stick of chalk. "Okay, class. Suggestions?"

Kenny Baldridge raised his hand.

"Venezuela," he said. "My grandpa is from there."

"Very good, Kenny. Would you like to tell us something about Venezuela?"

"They eat fried bananas," Kenny said.

"Very interesting," Ms. Schmidt said. "Let's find Venezuela on the map."

Leave it to Ms. Schmidt to turn the Third-Grade Olympics into school.

After we learned that Venezuela is in South America, Ms. Schmidt asked for more countries.

Travis Hoffberg said China.

Mary Grace said France.

Rose Marie Newman said Namibia.

Zachary said Madagascar.

Ms. Schmidt showed it to us on the map. It bugged me that Zachary hadn't made it up. I felt stupid that I'd never heard of it before.

I leaned over and whispered, "How do you even know about Madagascar?"

Zachary shrugged.

"I just know," he said. *"Everybody* knows."

Ms. Schmidt said, "I think we should take a vote. How many of you would like Room Six to represent Venezuela in the Third-Grade Olympics?"

A few people raised their hands. I sat on mine. I thought maybe Ms. Schmidt would make us eat fried bananas if we were Venezuela.

I voted for China. I could tell Zachary was mad. But I wasn't going to vote for a country just because it had good runners. Who cared about having good runners anyway?

All the girls except Rose Marie Newman voted with Mary Grace.

Room Six got stuck being France.

"*Magnifique!*" Ms. Schmidt clasped her hands together. "That means 'magnificent' in French."

Great, I thought. I may not have wanted to be Madagascar, but I didn't want to be France, either. If I knew Mary Grace, France was probably full of girls.

I leaned over to tell Zachary, but I stopped when I saw his face.

"You should have voted for Madagascar," he whispered.

•

On Friday, Mr. Hudson made us run twice around the playground.

I pretended to look for spiders, the way I always did, so everyone would think that was why I finished last.

"Listen up!" Mr. Hudson called. "Third-graders will compete in basketball, the long jump, jump rope, and the relay race."

Andrew clenched his fists in the air. "Basketball! Yes!" he yelled. "Room Six is the king of basketball!"

"Except for Mary Grace," Zachary said. "Don't forget. We have *her* on our team."

"I heard that, Zachary," Mary Grace said. "For your information, I am the best jump roper in the third grade. Maybe in the whole school."

"Who cares about jump rope?"
Zachary said.

"Also, for your information, you stink at jump rope," Mary Grace said.

"I've never even done it," Zachary mumbled. Mary Grace had told him off. Secretly, I was kind of glad.

"The Olympics won't be starting for two weeks," Mr. Hudson said. "That will give us plenty of time to prepare. And remember, you're a team! When one of you wins, you all win."

I raised my hand.

"Hey, what do we win?" I asked.

"At the end of the Olympics, there will be an awards ceremony," Mr. Hudson said. "The third-grade teachers and I will hand out medals and trophies."

Cool, I thought. A trophy for basketball would look great on my bookshelf, right next to my photograph of the Goliath bird-eater spider.

I had almost forgotten about the relay race. Almost. Until I heard Zachary whisper to Andrew, "Guess who's not going to win a trophy for running fast?"

3

Practice, Practice, Practice

I have never been a fast runner.
I don't know why. My mother says
I was always slow. She says I never
crawled much because I was too busy
trying to pick up the fuzz on the
carpet. Then I'd see a spider and
forget all about crawling.

Maybe if I'd practiced crawling
more, I'd have gotten faster at
running.

On Wednesday, Mr. Hudson said, "Today we'll practice jumping rope. On Friday, we'll work on basketball. The next Wednesday, we'll try the long jump. That Friday, we'll run relay races."

It was nice knowing that I didn't have to worry about running for nine whole days.

Now, the boys all stood in one clump, and the girls in another.

Mr. Hudson started off by asking, "How many of you think jumping rope is just for girls?"

All the girls raised their hands. All the boys raised theirs, except for Myron Petticord, who never pays any attention.

"Almost all of you, huh?" Mr. Hudson smiled. "Check this out."

He barely moved his arms.
He jumped so fast and low
that I couldn't see how
the rope made it under
his feet. It did, though.
He didn't mess up once.

"Cool," Travis Hoffberg
whispered.

After a couple of
minutes, Mr. Hudson
stopped jumping.

"That's hard work,"
he said, panting a little. "Whether
you're a boy or a girl."

He went over to a box and pulled
out some jump ropes.

"You'll have to take turns," he said.
"Let's see what you can do."

Jumping rope is harder than it
looks. None of the boys said so. We just

goofed around a lot so no one could see how lousy we were at doing it.

Finally, when I started whipping the jump rope over my head and tried to lasso Mary Grace, Mr. Hudson made us quit fooling around.

"Let's see some serious rope jumping," he said.

So we tried. Travis jumped four times before he tripped on the rope.

Andrew jumped six times. Zachary and I each jumped nine.

"Ha, ha," Mary Grace yelled from her clump of girls. "You boys!"

We practiced jumping rope for the rest of P.E. Andrew got up to ten jumps before tripping. Zachary got up to twelve. I got up to fourteen.

Practicing helped.

•

That Friday, Mr. Hudson said, "Time for basketball drills!"

"Hooray!" Zachary and Andrew and I yelled all together.

Regina Littlefield's eyes glittered. "Give me a ball," she said. "I'll show you how it's done!"

Regina is amazing at sports. Also at spitting.

Mr. Hudson divided us into two teams.

"In the Third-Grade Olympics, only nine of you will play at a time. We'll rotate everyone in so each of you will have a chance to play," he said.

I raised my hand. "Can't we just use the best players?" I asked.

"Remember what I said about being a team?" Mr. Hudson said.

"But Mr. Hudson!" Zachary said. "Mary Grace couldn't catch a basketball if I handed it to her. And her dribbling—"

"Listen, Zachary," Mary Grace said. "I bet you can't spell 'luscious.' I bet you can't even spell 'furnace.'"

Mary Grace is a really good speller.

"Hold it, campers," Mr. Hudson said. "We're a team. We play

together." Then he crossed his arms, and suddenly he looked serious. Like a regular teacher.

Even though I got stuck on the same team as Mary Grace, practice was fun. I am good at basketball. Mr. Hudson had Mary Grace and some of the other kids practice dribbling and shooting.

After fifteen minutes, Mary Grace finally got a basket. She bent her knees and tossed the ball in the air from underneath. I'm not even sure her eyes were open, but the ball swished through the net.

"Atta girl, Brennerman,"
Mr. Hudson said, high-fiving her.
Mary Grace was smiling like crazy.

She saw me watching. Her smile
started to fade away.

Then I did a really weird
thing.

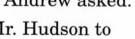

I gave her a thumbs-up.
I have no idea why I did it.
I guess I was thinking about
being a team.

Mary Grace smiled a little. Then
she turned around and went back to
throwing the ball and not making
baskets.

•

"Did you see Mary Grace trying to
pass that basketball?" Andrew asked.
We were waiting for Mr. Hudson to
walk us back to Room Six.

"I could glue it to her hands with rubber cement and she'd still drop it," Zachary said.

"She sure stinks at basketball," I said. I was relieved that they hadn't seen me give Mary Grace a thumbs-up.

But Zachary was looking at me funny.

"What?" I finally said.

He shook his head.

"She's not the only one who stinks at something," Zachary said.

4

And More Practice

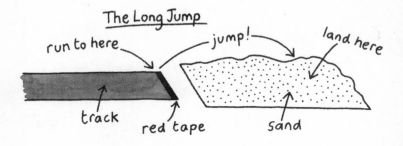

The next Wednesday was the long jump. I hadn't ever done a real long jump before. I'd done a lot of regular jumping, though. Plus all that jump roping. How hard could the long jump be?

Pretty hard, actually. There were all kinds of rules. You had to run up to a piece of red tape. But then your toes couldn't go over the tape. Then, when you got to the red tape, you had to jump as far as you could and land in a big pile of sand. The best part about long jumping was landing in that sand.

Regina Littlefield was the best long jumper in Room Six. She jumped eight feet, two inches. Rose Marie Newman was next best. She jumped seven feet, six inches. I was really surprised. I didn't think Rose Marie was any good at sports.

While we waited in line for our turn to run and jump, I saw something crawling in the grass and bent down to look.

"Hey, you guys!" I said. "Check out this spider!"

Andrew and Zachary got down on their knees with me.

"It's a cellar spider," I told them. "A lot of people think it's a brown recluse spider because of the markings on its back, but it's not."

"Brown recluse spiders aren't as cool as scorpions," Zachary said, standing up. "One time, in Maine, my dad almost ran over a scorpion in his car."

"You've told us about a million times," Andrew said.

"Did I tell you how my dad—?"

"Slammed on the brakes because he thought it was a squirrel? *Yes*," Andrew said.

"Because it was as big as a squirrel—"

"We *know*," Andrew said. "Enough already about the big scorpion."

screech!

"Anyway," I said, "there aren't any scorpions in Maine."

"Yeah," Andrew said.

"Even though there are fourteen hundred species of scorpions," I said.

"Really?" Andrew said. "Cool."

The line moved forward. I could feel Zachary's eyes staring at the back of my neck. It felt like he was drilling two holes into me with hot needles.

Finally he whispered, "You're not the only one who knows about things."

"I never said—"

"Besides," Zachary said, "I'd rather

be a fast runner than know things about stupid old spiders."

I turned around.

"Hey!" I yelled. I didn't like him calling spiders stupid. "I think—"

"Joey!" Mr. Hudson said. "Eyes forward, big guy!"

After another minute, I heard Zachary whisper, "Who cares what you think, anyway?"

•

Friday was running practice. I told Ms. Schmidt, "I think I have a fever."

I wasn't really lying. Being afraid feels like being sick.

"Let me feel your forehead, Joey," she said.

Uh-oh. I hate it when teachers do things moms are supposed to do.

"Well, you feel all right to me, Joey," Ms. Schmidt said. "But if you think you're sick, you can go to the office and call your mom."

I didn't want to go to the office. Then I'd have to sit with Ms. DiPesto, who answers the phones.

Ms. DiPesto knows my mom. Whenever I got sent to the office for doing something wrong, Ms. DiPesto would shake her head and say, "I remember when your mom used to give you baths in the sink."

"Can't I just sit out on the playground and watch?" I asked.

"If you feel well enough to do that, why don't you try to participate?" Ms. Schmidt asked. She leaned down close to me. "The Olympics start next week."

I nodded.

"Today Mr. Hudson's going to work with the class on relay racing," she said. "It might be fun."

I knew it would be awful. But I trudged out to the playground with everyone else.

I thought, I'm doomed.

•

Mr. Hudson divided Room Six into five teams. I was on a team with Travis Hoffberg, Regina Littlefield, Daniel Presley, and Xenia Zainer. Xenia's middle name was Yvette, so her initials were XYZ. That was the only interesting thing about her.

"Today we'll just practice racing

each other. In the real Third-Grade Olympics, the relay team you're on now will race a relay team from another third-grade class," Mr. Hudson explained. "The class—er, the country—that wins will be the one with the most relay teams that finish first."

It sounded complicated. For the first time I could remember, I didn't care about winning. All I cared about was not being the one who made us lose.

Regina kind of took over our team. "We need someone good at the beginning. Travis, you be our first runner," she said. Travis smiled and bowed.

"I'll be last," Regina said. "That way, if we're behind, I can catch up. You guys go in the middle." She meant Xenia and Daniel and me.

We all lined up. I was in between Xenia and Daniel. I didn't know Daniel very well. He was new. He was always getting a bloody nose and having to go to the office. I was glad he was there, though. Otherwise, Xenia and I would have been the only slow ones.

"Regina's kind of bossy, but she's fast," I said, just to make conversation.

Daniel nodded. He looked nervous.

He was wearing sandals. I only wear sandals at the beach.

I looked around, trying to find Zachary and Andrew. They had gotten on the same team. Andrew was at the front of their line. Zachary was at the back.

Andrew didn't see me, but Zachary did. He pointed at me and held his stomach, laughing.

I looked away.

•

We came in fourth out of five teams. Daniel lost one of his sandals. Xenia skipped the whole way. I tried really, really hard, but I don't think I did much better.

Regina was miserable.

"We stink," she said. "We totally stink."

"But Regina," Travis said, "everyone in the class is on the same team, remember? We're all France."

"Yeah, but OUR part of France stinks," Regina said. Then she started to get organized. "Listen, Daniel. You gotta get rid of those sandals. Don't you have any sneakers?"

Daniel shook his head. He looked terrified. No one had said so much to him at once all year.

"Well, get some," Regina said. "And Xenia. Stop skipping. This is a running race. You're supposed to run. Not *skip*."

"I wasn't skipping," Xenia said. "I was pretending to be a pony."

"Well, quit it," Regina said. "You can be a pony at recess. During Third-Grade Olympics, you have to be a runner."

Xenia looked pouty.

"I was going to braid my hair like a pony's mane," she said.

Regina looked disgusted. Then she looked at me, and her look changed. She looked like she felt sorry for me.

"I don't know what *you* should do, Spider," she said.

I looked down at my sneakers. I wished they were sandals. I wished that was the problem.

Regina sighed.

"Just run faster," she said.

5

Slow Spider

After school, Andrew and Zachary and I walked to Andrew's house to shoot hoops. Most days after school I get a ride home with Mary Grace, but on Fridays I always go to Andrew's.

Usually, just knowing that I didn't have to carpool with Mary Grace and her crazy little sister, Angela, would have made me happy. Today, though,

I almost wished I were going home with them.

We walked up Orchard Lane, Andrew bent over looking for pieces of dog doo with snail tracks on them, me looking for spiders. Zachary walked behind us, not looking for anything, not talking.

Finally he said, "It was pretty cool today, coming in first in relay races, huh, Andrew?"

"Yeah," Andrew said, still hunched over, hunting for dog doo.

"I love being fast like that," Zachary said.

I could hear the *slap slap* of his sneakers on the sidewalk.

"Winning," Zachary said. "Beating everyone."

"Uh-huh," Andrew said.

"Being the best," Zachary said. "Like the Yankees in the 2000 World Series. Like the Pacers in the 1999-2000 NBA Finals."

"Not the Pacers," I said. "The *Lakers*. The Lakers won the championship." Zachary didn't say anything. I could tell he was mad.

My heart was pounding. We turned onto Deer Hill Court.

"How'd you guys do?" Zachary asked. I knew he meant me.

"Fourth," I said.

"With Regina on your team?" Zachary asked.

"Yeah."

"Wow," Zachary said. "Then you must be really slow."

I was glad Zachary was behind me,

so he couldn't see my face.

He'd pulled a twig off a tree so he could scrape it against the Orsons' iron gate.

"Quit it, Zachary," Andrew said, finally straightening up.

"Yeah," I said. "Quit it."

I knew Zachary was picking on me about being a slow runner. He'd been doing it for days. I had no idea why. But suddenly, I didn't care about why. I was just sick of it.

"Okay, okay. I'm just saying that you're really, *really* slow," Zachary said. I could hear the twig plicking against the gate as we walked. "Right?"

I couldn't stand it anymore.

"So I'm slow," I said. "So I'm really slow. Maybe the slowest kid in the class. Maybe even slower than Mary Grace. So what? *So what?*"

I was really angry now. I was starting to scare myself. I turned around and Zachary almost walked right into me.

"At least I'm better than you at basketball and Capture the Flag. At least I know about spiders. At least I don't tell the same old scorpion story about a million times an hour." I was practically yelling. "At least I don't vote for Madagascar!"

At first I thought he was going to hit me with the stick. But he didn't. He just shook his head. "Dumb old Spider," he said. "You think you know everything just because you know about spiders."

"No, I don't!"

"You don't know everything," Zachary said. "You didn't even know that Madagascar was a real country."

"So?"

Zachary's eyes were tiny slits.

"Other people know stuff, too, you know," he said. "Stuff even you don't know."

I pushed past him, walking back the way we'd come. I could hear Andrew yelling for me, but I didn't even turn around.

6

Teamwork in the Teachers' Lounge

On Wednesday at breakfast, Mom asked, "Aren't you hungry, Joey?"

"No," I said. "I think I might be sick."

"Oh?" Mom sounded worried.

I tried to look pathetic.

"My stomach hurts," I said. Then

I got carried away. "I think I may have that disease where blood comes out of your eyes."

Mom crossed her arms over her chest. "Oh?"

"And after you're dead and they cut you open, your insides have turned to soup," I said.

I could tell I'd gone too far.

"Eat a bagel," Mom said. "It's good with soup."

I took a bite. Mom sat down across from me and took a sip of coffee. "What's up?" she asked.

"Nothing."

"How's school?"

"Fine." I took another bite of my bagel. "We have the Third-Grade Olympics today. We have to do running."

"Cool," Mom said.

"Not cool. I hate running. I stink at running." For a second, I thought I would cry.

"Oh, but honey," Mom said. "The Olympics aren't about winning. You know that, right?"

"Mr. Hudson keeps telling us that."

"Well, he's right," Mom said. "The Olympics are about trying your hardest. Anyway, at least Zachary and Andrew will be there to cheer you on."

"Not Zachary," I said. "Zachary hates me."

"He does not."

"He says I know too much," I said, not looking at her.

"Well," she said. "You can't know too much."

See? I said to Zachary in my head.

"Of course," Mom said, "there's a difference between knowing things and showing off that you know them."

"I don't show off!" I said, even though I knew she was right.

"I didn't say you did," Mom said. She stood up and gave me a kiss on the forehead. Then she wiped her mouth on the back of her hand. "Oops," she said. "Hope I don't catch that soup thing."

I smiled a little.

"I have to get Louise out of the bathroom," Mom said, heading for the stairs. Louise is my older sister. She is always in the bathroom.

"Remember," Mom said as she left the kitchen, "you just be the best friend you can be."

"I know," I said, but not loud enough so she could hear.

"All you can do is your best," Mom said from the hall.

●

At school, the third-grade teachers hung a huge banner between the two trees in the middle of the playground.

It said, "Everyone's a winner in the Third-Grade Olympics."

The fifth-grade band played the Olympic theme song that was always on television. Ms. Stone, the music teacher, flapped her arms and stomped her foot, but the Olympic theme song still sounded like "Old McDonald Had a Farm." Everyone clapped, anyway.

Ms. Elliot's class was Greece, which was the country that invented the Olympics millions of years ago. Mrs. Meredith's class was Ireland. All the kids in Mrs. Meredith's class wore green baseball caps for the Parade of

Countries. Mary Grace was jealous.

"We should have worn costumes," she said as we waited to walk around the playground in front of the first graders. "We could have worn those cute little French hats—berets."

"It's bad enough being France," I whispered back. "There's no way I would have worn a *little hat*."

Mr. Seelenbacker's class was Antarctica, which I could tell made Ms. Schmidt mad.

"Antarctica is not a country. It's a *continent*," she whispered to us about twenty times while we waited for them to walk around the playground.

Finally, it was our turn. All the little kids clapped and cheered. I spotted Ms. Levitsky, my old kindergarten teacher. She caught my eye and winked, which made me feel better.

But I was still feeling pretty sick.

Mr. Hudson handed out clipboards and whistles to all the third-grade teachers. Then he turned and faced the little kids.

"Okay, big guys," he said. "Today our third-grade athletes will compete in the jump rope. Let's cheer for all our competitors."

We all got two chances to jump rope for one minute. Mr. Seelenbacker held the stopwatch and recorded our best score.

It was a funny thing. It didn't even matter that Regina was a girl or that Mary Grace was Mary Grace. We all clapped for each other. I even yelled,

"Go, Regina!" when Regina got up to do her first jump. Then, after she'd jumped fifty-six times in one minute, I turned around and high-fived Andrew who was sitting right behind me.

Zachary and I didn't high-five, the way we would have done before. We looked at each other, though. It looked like Zachary kind of smiled.

"A personal best for Littlefield," Mr. Seelenbacker said happily.

I jumped forty-three times in one minute. Or maybe it was thirty-nine. I couldn't remember. It didn't really matter.

Regina came close, but Mary Grace was the best jumper in France, and France won the gold medal in jumping rope.

Jumping rope took all of
Wednesday. By Friday, it was time
for basketball.

Mr. Hudson picked countries out
of his baseball hat. France got to play
Antarctica first. Greece played
Ireland. The winners of each game
played each other for the gold medal.

I was glad about playing
Antarctica. Their best
player was
Rudy Pepperidge,
who had the
biggest head in the
third grade and was
definitely no match
for Regina. I thought our chances of
beating them were pretty good.

Mr. Hudson was the referee for

Greece and Ireland. He looked at his clipboard and said, "Anyone know where Ms. Schmidt is?"

Mary Grace raised her hand. "In the teachers' lounge," she said. She always kept track of teachers.

Mr. Hudson frowned. "She's supposed to referee the game—maybe she forgot." He checked his watch. "Hey, Joey and Zachary. Go get Ms. Schmidt."

Zachary and I looked at each other. Then we looked back at Mr. Hudson.

"You mean, go in the teachers' lounge?" I asked.

Mr. Hudson nodded impatiently. "Yeah, just knock first. They won't care. Tell them I'm looking for Liz...er, Ms. Schmidt."

Zachary and I started walking

toward the main hallway. "Run!" Mr. Hudson yelled. "Tell her we're waiting on her!"

So we ran. We stopped when we got to the hallway, because that's the rule. Zachary beat me. Of course. But he didn't say anything about it.

As we walked down the hallway, I said, "I think we're the first kids in the history of the school who get to go in here."

I waited to see if he would answer me or just look away.

"My dad went to this school, and he never got to see the teachers' lounge," Zachary said. "And that was back in the seventies. I have his old yearbook. You should see his hair."

The lounge was at the

end of a long, dark hallway. Today it seemed quiet and kind of spooky.

We stopped outside the door of the lounge. Zachary put up his hand to knock.

"Hey," I whispered. "If they let us in, you distract the teachers. I'll try and get a look in the closet."

Zachary's eyes got big. "Be careful, Spider."

I nodded back. I forgot all about the Olympics, about being a slow runner, about Zachary saying crummy things. I knocked on the door.

"Yes?" It was some lady, not Ms. Schmidt.

"Uh, it's Joey Storch. Is Ms. Schmidt in there?"

I could hear a lot of laughing and moving around.

"Come in, Joey," Ms. Schmidt said.

I pushed open the door, and Zachary and I stepped inside. The room had dirty yellow walls and a ratty couch. I could see a bulletin board with lots of announcements tacked onto it. The lady who'd answered when we'd knocked was Ms. DiPesto. She was on the couch drinking coffee. Mr. Scruggs, the janitor, was sitting next to her. He was eating a muffin.

Ms. Schmidt was standing at the coffee machine, pouring herself a cup. "Yes, boys?" she said.

"Uh, Mr. Hudson—" I started to say, but suddenly Zachary grabbed his stomach and bent over.

"Ow!" he yelled.

Ms. Schmidt set her coffee mug down. "Zachary?" she said.

Zachary yelled even louder. "Ow! *Ow!* My stomach!"

It sounded pretty real. I was impressed.

Everyone got up and ran toward us. They were all talking at once. Ms. DiPesto put her hands on Zachary's shoulders and tried to walk him to the couch. Mr. Scruggs kept calling him "son." Everyone looked worried.

While they were fussing and talking, I checked out the room. The closet door, painted green, was over by the window. I made sure no one was paying attention. I casually walked over to the door and stood in front of it. With my hands behind my back, I tugged on the door handle and felt it open. I looked over my shoulder and peeked inside.

The closet was empty, except for a broom and a cardboard box that had "coffee supplies" written in red pen across the front.

Aha, I thought. The box! I sniffed.

It didn't *smell* like dead kids.

Then I leaned in and pulled the cardboard flaps apart.

The box was empty. Rats, I thought.

"Joseph Storch!"

I jumped and turned around. Ms. Schmidt was staring at me.

"What are you doing in there?" she asked.

I thought fast. "Making sure there aren't any bombs," I said. "Criminals are always trying to blow up teachers."

I thought Ms. Schmidt would like me trying to protect the teachers.

"Just come out of there and close the door," Ms. Schmidt said.

Quickly I closed the door. Zachary

looked at me and smiled a little.

Ms. DiPesto was still fussing over Zachary, wondering if eight-year-olds got gallstones, when Zachary stood up.

"I feel better now," he said. "I feel all right."

"I don't know, Zachary," Ms. Schmidt said. "I think Ms. DiPesto should take you down to the office. Maybe we should call your mother."

"Oh, he's okay," I said. "He gets this all the time. It's just a cramp." I paused. "From being such a fast runner."

"Yeah," Zachary said. He looked at me. "That's all it is."

"Well ..." Ms. Schmidt still looked worried.

"Mr. Hudson needs you, Ms. Schmidt," I said. "You're supposed to be refereeing."

"Oh, my!" Ms. Schmidt put her arm up to her forehead. "I totally forgot!" She made her way to the door. Then she ran in a funny, grown-up way out to the playground. Zachary and I walked behind her.

"So?" Zachary said.

"Nothing," I said. "A broom and an empty box. Not even a tied-up garbage bag." After a minute I said, "You were right."

"I figured," Zachary said. "I figured it was just kids talking."

But it wasn't like he was bragging about being right.

"Yeah," I said, sighing. "Just kids acting like they know something when they don't."

Zachary nodded.

"Nobody knows everything," I said, not looking at him.

"Even really smart kids," Zachary said. "Even the kids other kids wish they were as smart as."

"Yeah," I said. "Even those smart kids act like jerks sometimes."

We could see Mr. Hudson and the kids clapping as Ms Schmidt ran out to the playground, her whistle bouncing against her chest.

"They don't mean to act like jerks," I said.

"Those other kids kind of know that," Zachary said.

7

On Your Marks ...
Get Set ...

France clobbered Antarctica, 20-14.
Regina and Zachary and I played the
best. Regina made nine baskets and
Zachary made six. I didn't make any,

but I passed a lot to Regina and Zachary. Plus I kept the ball away from Mary Grace.

"Quit it, Joey!" she yelled when I grabbed a ball that someone was throwing to her. But when I passed it to Zachary and he scored, Mary Grace whooped the loudest.

Next we clobbered Ireland, 22-17.

"France is on a roll!" Mr. Hudson said.

In the long jump, it was more of a struggle. Antarctica had some pretty good long jumpers. And Antarctica didn't have Mary Grace. In the end, Antarctica won the gold medal, and France won the silver.

"We should have won first place," Regina said, when Mr. Hudson couldn't hear. She hated losing.

"Nah, it's okay," I said. "That Rudy kid can jump."

"You'd think he wouldn't be able to get himself off the ground with that head," Regina said.

Finally it was time for the relay races.

Our relay team was racing a team from Greece. My heart felt like it was going to pound through my skin and fall on the playground right in front of my feet.

"On your marks," Mr. Hudson said, "get set ... GO!"

Travis started to run.

Please don't let me be slow, I thought.

I watched Travis touch the backboard at the end of the playground and start to head back.

He was ahead of the first runner from Greece. His hair was whipping through the air like a sail.

He crossed the finish line and Xenia began to run. I noticed that she'd pinned up her hair in a big purple hair bow. She wasn't skipping at all. By the time she hit the backboard, she was half a playground length ahead of Annie Gamble.

Please don't let me be slow.

She ran back toward me, and I took deep breaths and bent forward. I tried to think about what it would feel like to save the team, to run faster than any third-grade kid ever had in the whole history of third grade.

But all I could really hear was the
voice in my head.

Please don't let me be slow.

I ran as fast as I could. I know
I did that. My feet slapped the
pavement and my arms pumped back
and forth. I could hear my breathing
loud in my ears. The only thing louder
was the sound of Zachary cheering
back at the starting line.

In the end, I wasn't very fast.
Thatcher Albo started way after I did

and beat me by a mile. He beat me by so much that Daniel Presley started out behind, and not even Regina could win the race for us.

France came in third in the relay races. Ireland came in first.

But when we stood on the podium to get our medals, I was smiling.

I kept remembering the way they'd all cheered as I ran. Mary Grace and Andrew and Rose Marie and Zachary. Zachary most of all.

They'd cheered and yelled and hooted, and even when I'd come in way behind Thatcher Albo, they'd cheered some more.

I may not know everything. But I know they couldn't give me a medal as cool as that.

Don't forget to read ...

Spider Storch's
Teacher Torture

Spider Storch's
Carpool Catastrophe

Spider Storch's
Music Mess

Spider Storch's
Fumbled Field Trip

Spider Storch's
Desperate Deal

by Gina Willner-Pardo

illustrated by Nick Sharratt